From the Corner to the Clock
(A Fictional Memoir of Change)

Stan Scott

Copyright © 2024 by Stan Scott

All rights reserved.

This is a work of fiction. Names, characters, places, and incidents either are products of the author's imagination or are used fictitiously. Any resemblance to actual persons, living or dead, events, or locales is entirely coincidental.

Printed in the United States of America
10 9 8 7 6 5 4 3 2 1
ISBN: 9798329655681
Cover design by Stan Scott
Interior design by Stan Scott
By S Scott-Oakland California
Bysscottjr@gmail.com
Www.bysscott.org

For information about special discounts for bulk purchases, please contact Stan Scott
Special Sales at Bysscottjr@gmail.com
Foreword

Introduction: My Journey from the Corner to the Clock

Part I: Life on the Streets
1. Growing Up in the Hood: The Allure and Dangers of Street Life
2. The Hustle: Making Money by Any Means Necessary
3. Consequences: Brushes with the Law and Lost Opportunities
4. The Wake-Up Call: Realizing It's Time for a Change

Part II: The Transition
5. Letting Go: Cutting Ties with Negative Influences
6. Discovering Your Potential: Identifying Your Strengths and Passions
7. Education and Training: Acquiring the Skills for a Better Future
8. Networking: Building Connections and Finding Mentors
9. Overcoming Obstacles: Dealing with Setbacks and Self-Doubt

Part III: Embracing the 9 to 5 Life

10. Landing the Job: Resumes, Interviews, and Getting Hired

11. Adjusting to the Workplace: Professionalism, Ethics, and Office Politics

12. Managing Your Finances: Budgeting, Saving, and Investing

13. Work-Life Balance: Prioritizing Health, Family, and Personal Growth

14. Giving Back: Mentoring Others and Strengthening Your Community

Epilogue: Reflections on a Transformed Life

Resources and Recommended Reading

Acknowledgments

About the Man

Foreword

In the pages that follow, I take you on a deeply personal journey from the streets to the docks, a journey that is both inspirational and eye-opening. As a Labor Relations Representative for the Dock Workers Union (DWU) Local 100, I have become a pillar of my community, but my path to this position was far from easy.

My story begins as a casual worker on the waterfront, juggling two jobs while caring for my mother and pursuing an education at San Francisco City College to become an alcohol and drug counselor. It was during this challenging period that my health took a turn for the worse. A chronic smoker, my left lung collapsed due to fatigue and the toll of cigarettes. This health crisis forced me to confront the reality of my situation and make a choice: continue down a path of self-destruction or make a change for the better.

With the support of my doctors and a newfound determination, I chose the latter. After undergoing surgery to remove the damaged portion of my lung, I committed myself to a healthier lifestyle, walking daily to improve my lung capacity and overall well-being. It was during this period of recovery that I received a call from my coworkers about a promotion opportunity at the union. Seizing this chance, I returned to work, impressing my supervisors with my dedication and work ethic, even in the face of my recent health challenges.

My commitment to my own health and to my job did not go unnoticed. In April 2015, I received my partial membership into the DWU Local 100 Union as a longshoreman. Determined to make the most of this opportunity, I immediately joined the Steward Council, focusing on safety protocols, contract documents, and ensuring the well-being of my fellow union members. My dedication and leadership skills saw me rise through the ranks, serving as secretary and eventually chairperson of the Steward Council.

But my contributions to the community extend beyond my union leadership. In 2023, I began working with OSHA on Workers' Memorial Day, organizing an annual event at Middle Harbor Park to honor those who have lost their lives on the job. This powerful tribute has grown each year, with me pouring libations and union leadership reading the names of the fallen.

My journey is a testament to the power of resilience, hard work, and the transformative potential of organized labor. My story reminds us that no matter where we start in life, we have the capacity to change our circumstances and make a positive impact on those around us. As you read this book, I hope you will find inspiration in my words and the courage to face your own challenges head-on.

Stan Scott
Labor Assistance Professional

Introduction: My Journey from the Corner to the Clock

As I sit down to write this introduction, I find myself reflecting on the long and winding road that has brought me to this moment. It's a journey that began on the streets of Oakland, where I spent my youth caught up in the cycle of poverty, violence, and despair that traps so many young people of color. It's a journey that could have ended in tragedy, with my life cut short by a bullet or a prison sentence. But somehow, through a combination of luck, hard work, and the support of some incredible people, I found my way out of the darkness and into the light.

Today, I am a proud member of the Dock Workers Union (DWU) Local 100, working on the docks of the Port of Oakland. I am a husband, a father, and a community leader, dedicated to fighting for justice and opportunity for all people. And I am a writer, sharing my story in the hopes that it will inspire others to believe in the power of transformation and the possibility of a better world.

But my journey was not an easy one, and there were many times when I doubted whether I would make it out alive. Growing up in the flatlands of East Oakland, I was surrounded by poverty, drugs, and gang violence. My father and mother worked long hours just to keep a roof over our heads. As a young boy, I learned quickly that the streets were a dangerous place, and that if I wanted to survive, I would have to be tough, quick, and ruthless.

By the time I was a teenager, I was fully immersed in the street life. I was selling drugs, carrying guns, and running with a crew that was notorious for its violence and brutality. I had no hope for the future, no sense of purpose or direction.

All I knew was the code of the streets, the rush of power that came from being feared and respected.

But even in my darkest moments, there was a small part of me that knew I was meant for something more. I had always been smart and curious, with a love of reading and a talent for writing. I would sometimes sneak away to the library, losing myself in books about history, science, and far-off places. I dreamed of a life beyond the streets, even if I couldn't imagine how I would ever get there.

The turning point came when I was 19 years old. I had just been released from a short stint in county jail, and I was at a crossroads. I could either go back to the streets and risk getting killed or locked up for good, or I could try to find another way. That's when I met a man named Marcus, a former gang member who had turned his life around and become a community activist. Marcus saw something in me that I couldn't see in myself - a spark of potential, a hunger for something more. He took me under his wing, introduced me to books and ideas that opened my mind, and showed me that there was another path.

With Marcus's guidance and support, I started to turn my life around. I enrolled in community college, where I discovered a passion for social justice and a talent for leadership. I got involved in student government and community organizing, working to address issues like police brutality, gentrification, and educational inequity. I started to see myself not as a victim of my circumstances , but as an agent of change, with the power to shape my own destiny and make a difference in the world.

Fast forward a few years, and I found myself Standing on the docks of the Port of Oakland, a newly minted member of the DWU. It was a surreal moment, standing there in my hard hat and safety vest, looking out at the massive ships and cranes that stretched out to the horizon. I thought about how far I had come, from the street corners of East Oakland to the halls of higher education to the front lines of the labor movement. I thought about all the people who had helped me along the way - Marcus, my professors, my union brothers and sisters - and I felt a sense of deep gratitude and responsibility.

In the years since then, I have continued to grow and evolve, both personally and professionally. I have become a leader in my union, fighting for the rights and dignity of my fellow workers. I have become a mentor to young people in my community, sharing my story and my hard-earned wisdom in the hopes of inspiring them to dream big and persevere through adversity. And I have become a writer, using my words to give voice to the struggles and triumphs of my people, and to imagine a world where justice and opportunity are not just dreams but realities.

But through it all, I have never forgotten where I came from, or the lessons I learned on the streets. I have never forgotten the power of community, the importance of solidarity, or the transformative potential of education and organizing. And I have never forgotten the responsibility I bear, as someone who has made it out, to reach back and help others find their way.

That is what this book is about, at its core. It is about my journey from the corner to the clock, from the dead-end streets of East Oakland to the bustling docks of the Port. But more than that, it is about the journeys we all take, the obstacles we all face, and the choices we all must make. It is about the power of transformation, the resilience of the human spirit, and the unbreakable bonds of community and solidarity.

In the pages that follow, I will share my story in all its complexity and contradictions. I will take you with me on a journey through the streets and schools, the union halls and community centers, the victories and the setbacks that have shaped my life and my perspective. I will introduce you to the people and the ideas that have inspired me, challenged me, and sustained me through the darkest of times.

But I will also challenge you, dear reader, to think deeply about your own journey, your own struggles, and your own capacity for change. I will ask you to confront the systemic injustices and inequities that shape our society, and to imagine a world where every person has the opportunity to thrive and reach their full potential. I will invite you to join me in the hard but necessary work of building that world, brick by brick and block by block.

Because ultimately, this book is not just about my story. It is about our shared story, the story of a people and a nation still grappling with the legacy of slavery, segregation, and white supremacy. It is about the urgent need for a new kind of politics, a new kind of economy, and a new kind of society, one based on the values of justice, equity, and solidarity. And it is about the role that each of us can play, in our own lives and in our own communities, in bringing that vision to life.

So let us begin, you and I, on this journey of transformation and possibility. Let us walk together through the pages of this book, and through the streets and docks of Oakland, and let us see what we can learn, what we can build, and what we can become. Let us dare to dream of a better world, and let us have the courage to fight for it, today and every day.

With love and solidarity,
Stan

Part I: Life on the Streets

Chapter 1: Growing Up in the Hood: The Allure and Dangers of Street Life

I grew up in the heart of Oakland, California, in a neighborhood where the streets were more than just a means of getting from one place to another. They were a way of life, a culture that promised quick money, respect, and a sense of belonging. As a young man, I found myself drawn to this world, seduced by the idea of making a name for myself and providing for my family by any means necessary.

The hood was a place where survival was a daily struggle. Poverty, crime, and a lack of opportunities were the norm. Many of us felt like we had no choice but to hustle, to find ways to make money outside of the traditional job market. For some, that meant selling drugs, boosting cars, or engaging in other illicit activities. We justified our actions by telling ourselves that we were just doing what we had to do to get by.

Growing up, I watched as many of my friends and family members got caught up in the street life. Some ended up in prison, while others fell victim to violence or addiction. I saw firsthand the toll that this lifestyle could take on a person's mind, body, and spirit. But despite the risks, the allure of the streets was strong. The money, the respect, and the sense of power that came with being a player in the game were hard to resist.

As I got older, I found myself falling deeper into this world. I started hanging out with the wrong crowd, getting involved in things I knew were wrong but felt like I had no choice. I was living day-to-day, not thinking about the future or the consequences of my actions. All that mattered was surviving and making enough money to support myself and my family.

But even as I embraced the street life, there was a part of me that knew I wanted something more. I watched as some of my peers managed to escape the hood, either through education, hard work, or sheer determination. They showed me that there was another way, that I didn't have to be defined by my circumstances .

Still, making that change was easier said than done. The streets had a way of pulling you back in, even when you tried to leave. There were always new challenges, new temptations, and new obstacles to overcome. And when you're living in survival mode, it can be hard to think beyond the present moment.

Looking back, I realize that my experiences growing up in the hood shaped me in ways both good and bad.

They taught me resilience, resourcefulness, and the importance of looking out for the people you care about. But they also exposed me to a world of violence, addiction, and despair that no one should have to face.

In the chapters that follow, I'll share more about my journey from the streets to the docks, and the lessons I learned along the way. I'll talk about the challenges I faced, the people who helped me overcome them, and the work I'm doing now to give back to my community and help others find their own path to a better life.

But first, it's important to understand where I came from and the forces that shaped me. Because without that context, it's impossible to fully appreciate the transformation that took place in my life, and the hard-fought battles I had to wage to get to where I am today.

Chapter 2: The Hustle: Making Money by Any Means Necessary

In the world I grew up in, money was everything. It was the key to survival, respect, and power. If you didn't have it, you were nothing. And if you wanted it, you had to be willing to do whatever it took to get it.

For many of us, that meant hustling. Whether it was slinging dope on the corner, boosting cars, or running scams, we were always looking for ways to make a quick buck. We justified our actions by telling ourselves that we were just doing what we had to do to get by. In a world where legitimate opportunities were scarce, the hustle was often the only game in town.

I remember my first real taste of the hustle. I was 16 years old and hanging out with some older guys from the neighborhood. They were players in the game, always flashing cash and driving nice cars. I looked up to them, wanted to be like them.

One day, they put me up on a lick. We were going to boost some cars from a nearby dealership and sell them for parts. I was nervous as hell, but I didn't want to seem like a punk. So I went along with it.

We hit the dealership in the middle of the night, three of us working together to hotwire the cars and get them off the lot. It was a rush unlike anything I'd ever experienced before. The adrenaline, the sense of power, the knowledge that I was taking something that wasn't mine and getting away with it.

We made a few thousand dollars off that job, more money than I'd ever seen in my life. I felt like a king, like I was untouchable. Little did I know, that feeling wouldn't last.

As I got deeper into the hustle, I started taking bigger risks. I was selling drugs, running with a crew that was known for jacking people. I carried a gun everywhere I went, always on the lookout for the next score.

But the money I was making never seemed to last. No matter how much I brought in, there was always something else I needed to buy, some new expense I had to cover. I was living fast, blowing through cash as quickly as I could make it.

Looking back, I realize that the hustle was a trap. It promised quick money and an easy life, but in reality, it was a dead-end street. The more I hustled, the deeper I got into a world of violence, addiction, and despair. I was putting my life on the line every day, all for a few fleeting moments of glory.

But at the time, I couldn't see it. The hustle was all I knew, the only way I thought I could make it in this world. It wasn't until much later, when I hit rock bottom and had to confront the consequences of my actions, that I realized there had to be another way.

In the next chapter, I'll talk more about those consequences, and the events that finally forced me to wake up and start thinking about my future. But for now, it's important to understand the mindset that drove me to the hustle, and the powerful hold it had over my life for so many years.

Chapter 3: Consequences: Brushes with the Law and Lost Opportunities

As I fell deeper into the hustle, it was only a matter of time before I faced the consequences of my actions. I had my first brush with the law when I was 18. I was caught with a pocket full of dope and a gun in my waistband. I thought I was slick, thought I could talk my way out of it. But the cops weren't having it. They slapped the cuffs on me and hauled me off to jail.

I remember sitting in that holding cell, staring at the bars and thinking about how I'd messed up. I was looking at serious time, and I knew it. But even then, I couldn't bring myself to fully accept responsibility for my actions. In my mind, I was still the victim, still just doing what I had to do to survive.

That first arrest was a wake-up call, but it wasn't enough to make me change my ways. I got lucky with a lenient judge and was back on the streets in no time. But the experience had left a mark on me. I was more cautious now, more aware of the risks I was taking.

But the risks were always there, looming over me like a dark cloud. I lost count of the times I was pulled over by the cops, searched and questioned. Each time, I held my breath, wondering if this would be the time they found something that would put me away for good.

And it wasn't just the legal consequences I had to worry about. The street life was taking a toll on my personal life as well. I was losing friends to prison, to violence, to addiction. I remember getting the call about my boy J, how he'd been shot and killed in a drug deal gone wrong. I remember the hollow feeling in my chest as I stood over his casket, wondering if I'd be next.

But even with all that loss, all that pain, I still couldn't bring myself to walk away. The pull of the streets was too strong, the lure of easy money and respect too powerful. I told myself that I was different, that I was smarter than the rest. I convinced myself that I could keep playing the game without getting caught up in the consequences.

But the truth was, I was just fooling myself. Every day I spent hustling was another day I was risking my freedom, my future, and my life. I was missing out on opportunities, burning bridges with family and friends who wanted better for me.

It all came to a head when I caught my second case. This time, there was no lenient judge, no lucky break. I was facing years behind bars, and I knew I had no one to blame but myself.

Sitting in that courtroom, listening to the judge hand down my sentence, I felt a sense of despair wash over me. I had thrown my life away, all for a few fleeting moments of glory on the streets. I had let my family down, let myself down.

But even in that darkest moment, there was a glimmer of hope. As I was led out of the courtroom in handcuffs, I caught my parent's eye. My mother was crying, but there was something else in their gaze as well. A flicker of love, of belief. They hadn't given up on me, even when I had given up on myself.

That moment stayed with me as I began my sentence, a small spark of light in the darkness. And it was that spark that would eventually lead me to make the changes I needed to turn my life around.

But I'm getting ahead of myself. First, I had to hit rock bottom, had to lose everything before I could begin to build something new. In the next chapter, I'll talk about the wake-up call that finally made me realize it was time for a change.

Chapter 4: The Wake-Up Call: Realizing It's Time for a Change

I'll never forget the moment I realized I needed to change my life. I was sitting in my cell, staring at the cold, gray walls, when a guard came to tell me I had a visitor. I wasn't expecting anyone, so I was surprised to see my parents sitting on the other side of the glass.

They looked tired, worn down by the stress and heartache of seeing their son locked up. But there was something else in their eyes too, a fierce determination that I had never seen before.

"Stan," my father said, his voice cracking with emotion. "I can't watch you throw your life away like this. I won't. You're better than this, son. You've got so much potential, so much to offer the world. But you've got to be willing to change."

His words hit me like a punch to the gut. I felt tears welling up in my eyes, but I blinked them back, not wanting to show weakness. But the truth was, I was weak. I had been weak for a long time, too weak to break free from the grip of the streets.

But in that moment, something shifted inside me. I looked at my mother, saw the love and the pain in her eyes, and I knew I couldn't keep doing this to her. I couldn't keep doing this to myself.

"I'm sorry, Mama," I said, my voice barely above a whisper. "I'm so sorry. I want to change. I do. But I don't know how."

She reached out and put her hand on the glass, and I pressed my own hand against it, wishing I could feel her touch. "You start by making a decision," she said. "You decide that you want something better for yourself. And then you take it one day at a time. One step at a time. And you lean on the people who love you, the people who want to see you succeed."

I nodded, feeling a sense of determination rising up inside me. I knew it wasn't going to be easy. I knew I had a long road ahead of me. But for the first time in a long time, I felt like I had a reason to try.

That conversation with my parents was a turning point for me. It was the wake-up call I needed to start making changes in my life. But it was just the beginning.

When I got out of prison, I knew I couldn't go back to my old ways. I had to find a new path, a new way of living. But I also knew that I couldn't do it alone.

I started reaching out to people, asking for help. I went to job training programs, talked to counselors and mentors. I even started going to church, looking for a sense of community and purpose.

And slowly but surely, I started to build a new life for myself. It wasn't easy, and there were plenty of times when I wanted to give up. But every time I felt like I was slipping, I thought back to that conversation with my parents, to the love and belief in thier eyes.

I realized that I had been given a second chance, a chance to make something of myself. And I wasn't going to waste it.

In the next section of this book, I'll talk more about the steps I took to turn my life around. I'll share the story of how I went from a hustler on the streets to a longshoreman on the docks, and the lessons I learned along the way.

But the most important thing I want to convey is that change is possible. No matter how far gone you think you are, no matter how many mistakes you've made, there is always hope. There is always a way out.

You just have to be willing to take that first step.

Part II: The Transition

Chapter 5: Letting Go: Cutting Ties with Negative Influences

As I embarked on my journey of transformation, one of the first and most difficult steps was cutting ties with the negative influences in my life. This meant distancing myself from the people, places, and habits that had kept me trapped in the cycle of street life.

It was a painful process, as many of these individuals had been my friends, my partners in crime, my support system. We had been through so much together, and the thought of leaving them behind felt like a betrayal. But deep down, I knew that if I wanted to truly change my life, I had to surround myself with positivity and support.

I started by changing my phone number and deleting contacts from my old life. I knew that if I had easy access to these connections, the temptation to fall back into old patterns would be too great. It was a symbolic gesture, but it held real weight for me - a tangible sign of my commitment to moving forward.

Next, I had to confront the physical spaces that held negative associations. The street corners where I used to hustle, the trap houses where I'd spent countless hours - these were places I knew I could no longer frequent. It wasn't easy to navigate my neighborhood while avoiding these spots, but I found new routes, new hangouts, and gradually, the old haunts lost their pull on me.

Perhaps the most challenging aspect of this process was dealing with the reactions of those I was leaving behind. Some were understanding , recognizing that I was trying to better myself. Others felt abandoned, angry that I would turn my back on the life we'd shared. There were confrontations, attempts to pull me back in, and I had to stand firm in my resolve.

Throughout this period, I leaned heavily on the support of my family, particularly my father. He became my rock, my safe haven. When I was tempted to revert to old behaviors, I would think of his unwavering belief in me, and it would give me the strength to stay the course.

I also sought out new, positive influences. I started attending community events, volunteering, and connecting with people who were on a similar path of self-improvement. Slowly but surely, I built a new network, one that uplifted and inspired me.

Letting go of my old life was a gradual process, and there were times when I stumbled, when the pull of the familiar was almost too strong to resist. But each time, I picked myself up, reminded myself of the goals I had set, and kept pushing forward.

As I severed the ties to my past, I began to feel a sense of liberation. The weight of my old identity, the hustler, the criminal, started to lift. In its place, a new sense of self began to emerge - one filled with hope, potential, and the belief that I could be more than my past mistakes.

Cutting ties with negative influences was just the first step on my journey of transformation. But it was a crucial one, laying the foundation for all the growth and progress to come. In the next chapter, I'll delve into how I began to discover my own potential and passions, and how this self-discovery propelled me forward on my path to a new life.

Chapter 6: Discovering Your Potential: Identifying Your Strengths and Passions

As I worked to distance myself from the negative influences of my past, I found myself confronting a new challenge: figuring out who I was and what I wanted to do with my life. For so long, my identity had been tied to the streets, to the hustle. Without that, I felt lost, unsure of my place in the world.

I knew I needed to find a new direction, a new purpose. But where to start? I had no idea what I was good at, what I was passionate about. I had never given myself the space to explore these questions.

At first, I felt a sense of despair. I worried that I had wasted too much time, that it was too late for me to start over. But with the encouragement of my support system, particularly my mother and a few key mentors, I began to challenge these negative beliefs.

I started by taking a hard look at myself. What were my strengths? What did I enjoy doing? I thought back to my childhood, to the things that had brought me joy before the streets had taken hold. I remembered how much I loved to draw, how I would spend hours sketching superheroes and inventing my own comic book characters. I thought about the thrill I felt when I was able to help my younger siblings with their homework, breaking down complex concepts in a way they could understand .

These reflections gave me a glimmer of insight into my potential. But I needed more than just memories to guide me. I needed concrete tools and resources to help me discover my path.

I started by taking aptitude tests, assessments designed to identify my skills and interests. To my surprise, I scored high in areas like problem-solving, communication, and working with my hands. These results gave me a boost of confidence, a sense that I had valuable abilities to offer.

Next, I began to explore different hobbies and activities. I volunteered at a local community center, helping to organize events and mentor young people. I took a free art class at the library, rekindling my love for drawing and painting. I even joined a public speaking group, working to improve my communication skills.

Through these experiences, I started to develop a clearer sense of my passions and goals. I realized that I had a knack for leadership and a desire to give back to my community. I discovered that I loved the challenge of learning new things and pushing myself out of my comfort zone.

But perhaps the most important realization was that I had the power to shape my own future. My past did not define me, and my potential was not limited by my mistakes. I had the ability to learn, to grow, to become the person I wanted to be.

This shift in mindset was a turning point for me. Instead of dwelling on my regrets and shortcomings, I started to focus on my strengths and aspirations. I set goals for myself, both short-term and long-term, and began to work towards them with a new sense of determination.

Of course, this process of self-discovery was not always easy. There were times when I doubted myself, when I felt overwhelmed by the challenges ahead. But each small victory, each new insight into my potential, gave me the motivation to keep going.

As I continued to explore my passions and develop my skills, I began to see a path forward. I realized that I wanted to pursue a career where I could make a positive impact, where I could use my strengths to help others. And with this realization came a new sense of purpose and direction.

Discovering my potential was a journey of self-reflection, experimentation, and growth. It required me to let go of limiting beliefs and embrace the possibility of change. But through this process, I gained a deeper understanding of myself and what I was capable of achieving.

In the next chapter, I'll discuss how I began to translate this newfound self-awareness into concrete action, pursuing education and training to equip myself with the skills I would need to succeed in my new life.

Chapter 7: Education and Training: Acquiring the Skills for a Better Future

Armed with a new understanding of my strengths and passions, I knew that the next step in my journey was to acquire the knowledge and skills I would need to turn my aspirations into reality. This meant going back to school, something that felt both exciting and terrifying.

I hadn't been in a classroom in years, and the thought of starting over, of being surrounded by younger students who had never experienced the struggles I had faced, was daunting. But I knew that education was the key to unlocking the future I envisioned for myself.

I started by enrolling in a local community college. I met with an academic counselor who helped me identify the courses I would need to take to pursue my goals. I decided to focus on social work, drawn to the idea of helping others navigate the challenges of life.

At first, balancing school with my other responsibilities was a struggle. I was working part-time to support myself, and the demands of assignments and exams felt overwhelming at times. There were moments when I wanted to give up, when I doubted my ability to succeed in this new environment.

But I refused to let these obstacles derail me. I reached out to my professors, seeking their guidance and support. I formed study groups with my classmates, discovering the power of collaborative learning. And I leaned on my support system, particularly my mother, who cheered me on every step of the way.

As I progressed in my studies, I began to feel a sense of accomplishment and pride. I was mastering new concepts, developing critical thinking skills, and gaining a deeper understanding of the social issues I hoped to address in my future career.

But my education wasn't limited to the classroom. I also sought out practical training opportunities to complement my academic learning. I interned at a local social services agency, working directly with clients and learning the day-to-day realities of the field.

Through this hands-on experience, I gained valuable insights into the challenges and rewards of social work. I saw firsthand the impact that dedicated professionals could have on the lives of individuals and communities facing adversity.

As I neared the end of my degree program, I began to feel a new sense of direction and purpose. I had a clear vision for my future, a career path that would allow me to make a meaningful difference in the world.

But I also realized that my education was just the beginning. To truly succeed in my chosen field, I would need to continue learning and growing, staying up-to-date with best practices and emerging trends.

This realization instilled in me a lifelong commitment to learning. Even as I prepared to graduate and enter the workforce, I knew that I would never stop seeking out new knowledge and skills.

Looking back, I can see how my decision to pursue education was a pivotal moment in my journey of transformation. It opened up new opportunities, broadened my horizons, and gave me the tools I needed to build a better future for myself and those around me.

But education alone wasn't enough. To truly succeed in my new life, I would also need to build relationships, to connect with others who could offer guidance, support, and opportunities. In the next chapter, I'll explore the role that networking played in my transition, and how the power of human connection helped me navigate the challenges of starting over.

Chapter 8: Networking: Building Connections and Finding Mentors

As I progressed through my education and training, I began to understand that my success would depend not only on my own efforts but also on the relationships I built along the way. Networking, a concept that had once seemed foreign and intimidating to me, became a crucial part of my personal and professional growth.

At first, I was hesitant to reach out to others, feeling like an imposter in my new world. But I soon realized that most people were more than willing to offer guidance and support to someone who showed genuine interest and dedication.

I started by connecting with my classmates and professors, participating actively in discussions and seeking out opportunities to collaborate on projects. These interactions not only deepened my understanding of the material but also helped me build a reputation as a committed and capable student.

As I gained confidence, I began to expand my network beyond the classroom. I attended industry events and conferences, introducing myself to professionals in my field and learning about their experiences and insights. I joined professional organizations and volunteered for committees, taking on leadership roles that allowed me to develop new skills and make valuable contributions.

Through these efforts, I began to form meaningful connections with people who would play pivotal roles in my journey. One such person was a professor who had become a trusted mentor. She recognized my potential and took me under her wing, offering guidance on everything from coursework to career planning.

Under her mentorship, I gained a deeper understanding of the social work field and the challenges and opportunities that lay ahead. She encouraged me to pursue advanced education, helping me navigate the application process for graduate programs and providing letters of recommendation that spoke to my strengths and potential.

Another key connection was a supervisor from my internship who saw promise in my work and offered me a job upon graduation. This opportunity was a testament to the power of networking and the importance of making a positive impression in every interaction.

As I transitioned into my new role, I continued to prioritize building and maintaining professional relationships. I sought out mentorship from experienced colleagues, learning from their successes and challenges. I also made a point of connecting with other young professionals, creating a support system of peers who were navigating similar stages of their careers.

But my networking efforts weren't just about advancing my own interests. I also discovered the joy and fulfillment that came from being a mentor and advocate for others. As I gained experience and credibility in my field, I made a conscious effort to pay forward the support and guidance I had received.

I began to mentor students and young professionals, sharing my own experiences and offering advice on everything from job searching to work-life balance. I also became an active advocate for fatherhood and families in my field, working to create opportunities for underrepresented groups and challenging systemic barriers to success.

Through these efforts, I discovered that networking wasn't just about building transactional relationships for personal gain. It was about fostering a sense of community, a shared commitment to growth, learning, and positive change.

Looking back, I can see how the connections I made during my transition were instrumental in shaping my path forward. They provided me with knowledge, opportunities, and support that I could not have achieved on my own. And they inspired me to be a force for good in my own right, using my platform and influence to lift up others.

As I moved into the next phase of my journey, I carried these lessons with me. I knew that no matter what challenges lay ahead, I had a network of supporters and collaborators who would be there to help me navigate the way.

In the next chapter, I'll delve into some of those challenges, exploring the obstacles and setbacks I faced as I worked to build a new life and career. But I'll also share how the resilience and determination I had developed, along with the support of my network, helped me persevere and ultimately triumph.

Chapter 9: Overcoming Obstacles: Dealing with Setbacks and Self-Doubt

As I embarked on my new career path, I quickly learned that the road to success was not a smooth one. Despite my education, training, and growing network, I faced numerous obstacles and setbacks that tested my resolve and made me question my abilities.

One of the biggest challenges I faced was the job search process. Even with the support of my mentors and the promise of a job from my internship supervisor, I found myself struggling to secure a position that aligned with my goals and values. I sent out countless applications, attended numerous interviews, and faced rejection after rejection.

Each rejection felt like a personal failure, a sign that I wasn't good enough or that I had made a mistake in choosing this path. I began to doubt myself, wondering if I had what it took to succeed in this field.

But I refused to give up. I leaned on my support system, seeking encouragement and advice from my mentors and peers. They reminded me that setbacks were a normal part of the process and that each rejection was an opportunity to learn and grow.

I also took a proactive approach to my job search, seeking out feedback from interviewers and using it to improve my skills and presentation. I volunteered for additional projects and responsibilities at my internship, building my experience and demonstrating my value as a potential employee.

Eventually, my persistence paid off. I landed a position at a respected social services agency, working with a team of dedicated professionals to support individuals and families in need.

But the challenges didn't end there. As I settled into my new role, I encountered difficult clients, bureaucratic obstacles, and the emotional toll of working with people in crisis. There were days when I felt overwhelmed, when I questioned whether I had the strength and resilience to continue in this field.

In these moments, I drew on the lessons I had learned throughout my journey. I reminded myself of the progress I had made, the skills I had acquired, and the impact I was having on the lives of those I served. I sought support from my colleagues and supervisors, learning from their experiences and leaning on their expertise.

I also learned to prioritize self-care, recognizing that I couldn't pour from an empty cup. I made time for activities that brought me joy and helped me recharge, whether it was spending time with loved ones, pursuing a hobby, or simply taking a moment to breathe and reflect.

As I navigated these challenges, I began to develop a new sense of resilience and adaptability. I learned to embrace setbacks as opportunities for growth, to find creative solutions to problems, and to maintain a positive outlook even in the face of adversity.

I also learned to be kind to myself, to acknowledge my own humanity and the fact that perfection was an unrealistic expectation. I celebrated my successes, no matter how small, and used them as motivation to keep pushing forward.

Over time, I began to see the fruits of my labor. I developed a reputation as a skilled and compassionate social worker, earning the respect of my colleagues and the trust of my clients. I took on leadership roles within my organization, mentoring new staff members and advocating for systemic changes to better serve our community.

Looking back, I can see how the obstacles and setbacks I faced were essential to my growth and development. They taught me the importance of perseverance, adaptability, and self-reflection. They helped me build a strong foundation of resilience that would serve me well throughout my career and my life.

As I moved forward, I knew that there would be more challenges ahead. But I also knew that I had the tools, the support, and the inner strength to overcome them. And with each obstacle I faced, I grew more confident in my ability to navigate the complexities of my chosen path and to make a meaningful difference in the world.

In the next part of my story, I'll explore how I took the lessons and experiences of my transition and applied them to my new life as a working professional. I'll share the triumphs and the continued growth that came with embracing my purpose and living out my passion in service to others.

Part III: Embracing the 9 to 5 Life

Chapter 10: Landing the Job: Resumes, Interviews, and Getting Hired

After months of hard work, dedication, and personal growth, I finally felt ready to fully embrace the 9 to 5 life. Armed with my education, skills, and a newfound sense of purpose, I began the process of searching for a job that aligned with my goals and values.

I started by crafting a resume that highlighted my strengths, experiences, and accomplishments. I emphasized my academic achievements, internship experience, and the skills I had developed through my personal journey. I tailored my resume to each position I applied for, ensuring that I was showcasing the most relevant aspects of my background.

Next, I focused on preparing for job interviews. I practiced answering common interview questions, honing my ability to articulate my experiences and qualifications in a clear and compelling way. I also researched the organizations I was interested in, learning about their mission, values, and the specific challenges and opportunities they faced.

As I began to land interviews, I drew on the confidence and self-awareness I had cultivated throughout my journey. I approached each interview as an opportunity to share my story and my passion for making a positive impact. I was honest about my past struggles and how they had shaped me, but I also emphasized the growth and resilience I had developed as a result.

I remember one particularly pivotal interview with a community-based organization that focused on providing support services to at-risk youth. As I sat across from the hiring manager, I felt a deep sense of connection to their mission. I shared my own experiences growing up in a challenging environment and how those experiences had fueled my desire to give back and support others facing similar struggles.

The hiring manager was impressed by my authenticity and my clear commitment to the work. She saw in me not just a set of qualifications, but a person with a unique perspective and a deep understanding of the challenges their clients faced.

A few days later, I received the call I had been hoping for: I was offered the job. I felt a rush of emotion - excitement, gratitude, and a sense of profound accomplishment. I knew that this was more than just a job; it was an opportunity to put my skills and experiences to work in service of a cause I believed in deeply.

As I settled into my new role, I found that the transition to the 9 to 5 life was not without its challenges. I had to adjust to a new schedule, new responsibilities, and a new set of expectations. There were days when I felt overwhelmed or unsure of myself, when the weight of the work felt heavy on my shoulders.

But I also discovered a deep sense of fulfillment and purpose in my work. Every day, I had the opportunity to make a tangible difference in the lives of the young people I served. I could see the impact of my efforts in their smiles, their progress, and the hope that began to take root in their lives.

Over time, I began to thrive in my new environment. I built strong relationships with my colleagues, learning from their experiences and collaborating to develop innovative solutions to the challenges we faced. I took on additional responsibilities and leadership roles, growing in my skills and confidence.

And as I looked back on my journey - from the streets to the classroom to the office - I felt a profound sense of pride and gratitude. I had overcome so many obstacles, both internal and external, to get to where I was. I had proven to myself and to others that change was possible, that a person's past did not have to define their future.

Landing the job was a crucial step in my journey, but it was only the beginning. In the chapters to come, I'll explore the ongoing challenges and triumphs of embracing the 9 to 5 life - from navigating workplace dynamics to finding work-life balance to continuing to grow and make a difference in the world.

Chapter 11: Adjusting to the Workplace: Professionalism, Ethics, and Office Politics

As I settled into my new role, I quickly realized that succeeding in the 9 to 5 world required more than just the right qualifications and a strong work ethic. I had to learn to navigate the complex dynamics of the workplace, from the unwritten rules of office culture to the delicate balance of professional relationships.

One of the first challenges I faced was adapting to the norms and expectations of professional communication. Having come from a background where directness and informality were the norm, I had to learn to moderate my language and tone to fit the context of the workplace. I watched how my colleagues interacted, noting the way they framed feedback, handled disagreements, and presented themselves in meetings.

I also had to be mindful of the power dynamics at play in the office. As a new employee, I was acutely aware of the hierarchy and the importance of building positive relationships with my supervisors and colleagues. I made a point of being respectful, responsive, and willing to go the extra mile to support the team.

However, I also learned that office politics could be a tricky landscape to navigate. There were times when I witnessed or experienced conflicts, alliances, and subtle forms of discrimination that weren't always easy to address head-on. In these moments, I had to draw on my emotional intelligence and my commitment to my own values to find a way forward.

I remember one incident where a colleague made a dismissive comment about a client's background, implying that their struggles were a result of personal failings rather than systemic barriers. As someone who had faced my own share of prejudice and adversity, I felt a pang of frustration and anger.

But rather than lashing out, I took a deep breath and approached the colleague privately. I shared my own story and my perspective on the complexities of the issues our clients faced. I emphasized the importance of empathy and understanding in our work, and the need to challenge our own biases and assumptions.

To my surprise, the colleague was receptive to the conversation. They acknowledged their blind spots and expressed a willingness to learn and grow. That moment taught me the power of leading with compassion and the potential for honest dialogue to bridge divides.

As I navigated these dynamics, I also had to grapple with ethical questions and dilemmas that arose in the course of my work. Working with vulnerable populations, there were times when I had to balance my desire to help with the need to maintain professional boundaries and respect client autonomy.

I leaned heavily on the ethical training I had received and the guidance of my supervisors and mentors. I learned to document my decisions carefully, to seek out multiple perspectives, and to prioritize the well-being and self-determination of those I served.

Over time, I began to find my footing in the workplace. I developed a reputation as a reliable, principled, and compassionate colleague. I built strong relationships with my team members and earned the trust of my supervisors.

But I also realized that adjusting to the workplace was an ongoing process. As I took on new roles and responsibilities, I had to continue to adapt, learn, and grow. I had to stay attuned to the ever-shifting dynamics of the office and the broader field, and to find ways to stay true to my values while navigating the realities of the professional world.

Looking back, I can see how the challenges of adjusting to the workplace were an essential part of my growth and development. They taught me the importance of emotional intelligence, adaptability, and integrity. They helped me build the skills and relationships that would serve me well throughout my career.

And as I moved forward, I knew that the lessons I had learned about professionalism, ethics, and office politics would be invaluable as I took on new challenges and pursued my goals of making a difference in the world.

Chapter 12: Managing Your Finances: Budgeting, Saving, and Investing

As I settled into my new career and started earning a steady income, I quickly realized that managing my finances was a crucial aspect of building a stable and fulfilling life. Having come from a background where money was often scarce and unpredictable, I knew that I had a lot to learn about budgeting, saving, and investing.

I started by educating myself on the basics of personal finance. I read books, attended workshops, and sought advice from trusted mentors who had experience navigating the financial landscape. I learned about the importance of creating a budget, tracking my expenses, and living within my means.

One of the first steps I took was to sit down and create a comprehensive budget. I listed out all of my income sources and fixed expenses, such as rent, utilities, and student loan payments. I then allocated funds for variable expenses like groceries, transportation, and entertainment. Seeing all of my financial commitments laid out clearly helped me identify areas where I could cut back and redirect funds towards my savings and investment goals.

I also made a commitment to paying myself first. Before I spent money on anything else, I made sure to set aside a portion of my income into a savings account. I started small, with just a few percent of my paycheck, but as I adjusted to my new budget, I gradually increased that amount. Over time, I watched my savings grow, providing me with a sense of security and the freedom to make choices about my future.

As I got a handle on my day-to-day finances, I began to think more long-term. I knew that I wanted to build wealth and create financial stability for myself and my future family. I started researching investment options, learning about the power of compound interest and the importance of diversification.

I decided to start with a simple approach, opening a retirement account through my employer and allocating a portion of each paycheck towards it. I also opened a brokerage account and began investing in a mix of low-cost index funds and individual stocks. I knew that investing carried risks, but I also understood that over the long term, the stock market had historically provided strong returns.

As I watched my investments grow, I felt a sense of empowerment and pride. I was taking control of my financial future, creating opportunities for myself that I had never thought possible. But I also knew that managing my finances was an ongoing process, one that required discipline, learning, and adaptability.

There were times when unexpected expenses arose or when I was tempted to splurge on something I couldn't really afford. In those moments, I had to draw on the habits and mindset I had developed, reminding myself of my long-term goals and the importance of staying the course.

I also learned to be generous with my resources, both in terms of my time and my money. As I became more financially stable, I made a point of giving back to the communities and causes that mattered to me. I volunteered my skills, made charitable donations, and looked for ways to use my privilege and platform to make a positive impact.

Over time, I began to see the tangible results of my efforts. I was able to pay off my student loans, build up a robust emergency fund, and even start saving for a down payment on a house. I felt a sense of security and freedom that I had never experienced before, knowing that I had the resources to weather tough times and pursue my dreams.

Looking back, I can see how learning to manage my finances was a pivotal part of my journey. It taught me the power of discipline, planning, and long-term thinking. It gave me the foundation to build a life that was not only financially stable, but also deeply fulfilling and purposeful.

And as I moved forward, I knew that the lessons I had learned about budgeting, saving, and investing would continue to serve me well, enabling me to make a difference not only in my own life, but in the lives of those around me.

Chapter 13: Work-Life Balance: Prioritizing Health, Family, and Personal Growth

As I dove into my new career and took on increasing responsibilities, I found myself grappling with the challenge of maintaining a healthy work-life balance. The demands of my job, while fulfilling, could also be all-consuming, leaving little time and energy for other important aspects of my life.

I had always prided myself on my strong work ethic and dedication, but I soon realized that burning the candle at both ends was not sustainable. I started to experience the physical and emotional toll of long hours, high stress, and neglecting my own needs.

I remember one particularly challenging period when I was working on a major project with a tight deadline. I was putting in long hours at the office, skipping meals, and cutting back on sleep. I told myself that this was just a temporary sacrifice, that I would make up for it once the project was complete.

But as the weeks wore on, I found myself feeling increasingly exhausted, irritable, and disconnected from the people and activities that brought me joy. I was snapping at my loved ones, canceling plans with friends, and feeling like I was losing touch with the passions and hobbies that had once been so important to me.

It was a wake-up call that I couldn't ignore. I realized that if I wanted to sustain my success and happiness in the long run, I needed to make some changes. I needed to find a way to prioritize my health, my relationships, and my personal growth alongside my career.

I started by setting clear boundaries around my work time. I communicated with my team about my availability and the importance of disconnecting outside of work hours. I began to delegate tasks more effectively and to say no to projects or commitments that would push me beyond my limits.

I also made a commitment to prioritizing my physical and mental health. I started blocking off time in my schedule for exercise, meditation, and other self-care practices. I made sure to take my lunch breaks, to step away from my desk for short walks or stretches, and to get enough sleep each night.

As I made these changes, I started to feel a shift in my energy and perspective. I was more focused and productive during my work hours, and I had more capacity to be present and engaged in my personal life. I found myself looking forward to my hobbies and social activities again, and I was able to show up as a better partner, friend, and family member.

But finding work-life balance wasn't just about making time for myself. It was also about surrounding myself with a supportive community and aligning my career with my values and life goals.

I started to seek out colleagues and mentors who shared my commitment to balance and well-being. We traded tips and strategies, held each other accountable, and celebrated each other's successes both in and out of the office. I also got involved in employee resource groups and wellness initiatives, helping to create a workplace culture that valued and prioritized self-care.

At the same time, I began to reflect more deeply on how my work aligned with my personal mission and values. I asked myself tough questions about whether my job was truly fulfilling me, not just professionally but also personally. I started to explore ways to incorporate more of my passions and interests into my work, whether through volunteering, pro bono projects, or creative collaborations.

Over time, I found that prioritizing work-life balance not only made me happier and healthier, but also a better, more effective professional. When I was taking care of myself and feeling fulfilled in my personal life, I was able to bring my full self to my work. I was more creative, more resilient, and more able to make a positive impact on the people and causes I cared about.

Looking back, I can see how learning to prioritize work-life balance was a critical part of my journey. It taught me the importance of self-care, boundaries, and alignment. It showed me that success isn't just about climbing the ladder, but about creating a life that is rich, balanced, and meaningful.

And as I moved forward, I knew that the lessons I had learned about work-life balance would continue to guide me, helping me to stay grounded, focused, and fulfilled no matter what challenges and opportunities lay ahead.

Chapter 14: Giving Back: Mentoring Others and Strengthening Your Community

As I settled into my role as a longshoreman and found my footing in the 9 to 5 life, I began to feel a growing sense of responsibility to give back to my community. I knew firsthand the challenges and obstacles that many young people from backgrounds like mine faced, and I wanted to use my experiences and my platform to make a positive impact.

One of the first ways I got involved was through mentoring. I reached out to local youth organizations and offered to volunteer my time as a mentor and role model. I was paired with a teenage boy named Jamal who reminded me a lot of myself at that age - smart, ambitious, but struggling to find his way in a world that often felt stacked against him.

Jamal and I met regularly, talking about everything from school and family to his dreams for the future. I shared my own story with him, the ups and downs of my journey from the streets to the docks. I listened to his struggles and offered guidance and support where I could. But more than anything, I tried to show him that change was possible, that he had the power to shape his own destiny.

As I watched Jamal grow and thrive under my mentorship, I felt a deep sense of fulfillment. I saw in him the same potential that others had seen in me, and I was determined to help him unlock it. And as word of my mentoring spread, I found myself taking on more and more mentees, each one a reminder of the impact that one person can have.

But my involvement didn't stop with mentoring. I also became active in my union, the DWU Local 100, advocating for the rights and well-being of my fellow workers. I joined committees focused on safety, training, and community outreach. I spoke up about the importance of fatherhood and families on the docks, pushing for policies and practices that would create more opportunities for people from all backgrounds.

As I took on more leadership roles within the union, I also started to think more broadly about the systemic issues affecting my community. I saw how the lack of access to quality education, healthcare, and job opportunities was holding back so many young people from reaching their full potential. I knew that mentoring and individual support, while important, could only go so far in addressing these deeper challenges.

So I started to get involved in local politics and advocacy work. I attended community meetings, spoke at rallies, and met with elected officials to push for policies that would invest in underserved neighborhoods and create more pathways to success. I used my story as a testament to the power of second chances and the importance of building a more just and equitable society.

Through all of this work, I found that giving back was not a one-way street. The more I invested in my community, the more I gained in return. I built deep, meaningful relationships with the people I served and the colleagues I worked alongside. I gained new skills and perspectives that enriched my own life and work. And I felt a profound sense of purpose and fulfillment, knowing that I was part of something bigger than myself.

As I reflect on my journey and look to the future, I know that giving back will always be a central part of my life. Whether through mentoring, union leadership, or community advocacy, I am committed to using my voice and my resources to lift up others and strengthen the bonds of our shared humanity.

And I hope that my story can serve as an inspiration to others, a reminder that no matter where we come from or what obstacles we face, we all have the power to make a difference. By investing in our communities and in each other, we can build a world where every person has the opportunity to thrive and reach their full potential.

Epilogue: Reflections on a Transformed Life

As I sit here today, looking back on my journey from the corner to the clock, I am filled with a profound sense of gratitude and awe. If you had told me 20 years ago that I would one day be a respected leader in my union, a sought-after mentor and advocate, and a voice for change in my community, I would have laughed in disbelief. But here I am, living proof that transformation is possible, that our pasts do not have to define our futures.

When I think about the person I was back then - the hustler, the addict, the lost soul - it feels like a lifetime ago. The road from there to here has been long and winding, filled with obstacles, setbacks, and moments of doubt. There were times when I wanted to give up, to fall back into old patterns and surrender to the pull of the streets. But something kept me pushing forward - a spark of hope, a glimmer of possibility, and the unwavering support of the people who believed in me even when I didn't believe in myself.

As I've navigated this journey of transformation, I've learned so many lessons - about resilience and redemption, about the power of education and opportunity, about the importance of community and connection. I've learned that change is hard, but it's also possible. That our struggles can be our greatest teachers, if we're willing to listen and learn. And that the most meaningful successes are not the ones we achieve for ourselves, but the ones we create for others.

Looking back, I can see how each step of my journey - from the streets to the classroom, from the docks to the halls of power - has shaped me into the person I am today. My experiences have given me a unique perspective and a deep empathy for those who are struggling. They've taught me the value of hard work, perseverance, and second chances. And they've shown me that true leadership is about service, about using our gifts and our platform to lift up others and make a positive impact in the world.

As I move forward, I know that my journey of transformation is far from over. There will always be new challenges to face, new opportunities to grow, and new ways to give back. But I also know that I am not alone on this path. I am surrounded by a community of people who share my values and my vision, who are working tirelessly to create a more just and equitable world.

To anyone who may be reading this, facing their own struggles and doubts, I want to offer a message of hope and encouragement. Your past does not define you. Your mistakes do not diminish your worth. You have the power to change your story, to create a life of purpose and meaning. It won't be easy, and it won't happen overnight. But with hard work, determination, and the support of those who believe in you, anything is possible.

As I reflect on my own transformed life, I am filled with a sense of purpose and possibility. I know that my work is not done, that there is always more to learn, more to give, more to achieve. But I also know that I am exactly where I am meant to be, doing exactly what I am meant to do. And for that, I am deeply grateful.

To all those who have been a part of my journey - my family and friends, my mentors and colleagues, the young people I have had the privilege to serve - thank you. Your love, your wisdom, and your belief in me have been the greatest gifts of my life. And to all those who are still finding their way, know that you are not alone. Keep pushing forward, keep believing in yourself, and keep reaching for the life you deserve.

The journey of transformation is never easy, but it is always worth it. And I am living proof that no matter where you start, no matter what obstacles you face, you have the power to create a life of meaning, purpose, and profound beauty. So keep going, keep growing, and never give up on yourself or your dreams. The world needs your light, your gifts, and your unique contribution. And I can't wait to see the incredible impact you will make.

Resources and Recommended Reading

If you're looking to learn more about the themes and topics explored in this book, or if you're seeking guidance and inspiration for your own journey of transformation, here are some resources and recommended readings to check out:

Books:
1. "The Other Wes Moore" by Wes Moore - A powerful memoir that explores the divergent paths of two men with the same name, and the impact of choices, support, and opportunity.
2. "The New Jim Crow" by Michelle Alexander - A groundbreaking look at the racial disparities in the American criminal justice system and the impact of mass incarceration on communities of color.
3. "The Power of Habit" by Charles Duhigg - A fascinating exploration of the science of habit formation and change,

with practical strategies for transforming your life.

4. "Man's Search for Meaning" by Viktor E. Frankl - A classic work on finding purpose and resilience in the face of adversity, based on the author's experiences in Nazi concentration camps.

5. "The 7 Habits of Highly Effective People" by Stephen Covey - A comprehensive guide to personal and professional development, with a focus on principles of effectiveness and integrity.

6. Mobilizing in Our Own Name: Million Worker March: An Anthology by Clarence Thomas

7. Cleophas Williams: My Life Story in the International Longshore & Warehouse Union Local 10: An Introduction by Clarence Thomas

Organizations: 1. The Innocence Project - A nonprofit legal organization that works to exonerate wrongly convicted individuals through DNA testing and criminal justice reform.

2. The Last Mile - A nonprofit that provides technology training and job placement for individuals impacted by incarceration.

3. The Sentencing Project - A research and advocacy organization working to reduce racial disparities in the criminal justice system and promote alternatives to incarceration.

4. The National Mentoring Partnership - A national organization that provides resources and support for mentoring programs and relationships.

5. The Ella Baker Center for Human Rights - A nonprofit that advocates for racial and economic justice through community organizing, policy reform, and leadership development.

6. M3- Mentoring Men's Movement - A community re-entry organization that starts during incarceration to build a bridge back to the community with guidance and support upon release. It seeks to build healthier and safer communities through transitional and transformative services to the incarcerated, previously incarcerated, and others who are committed to positive change.

Podcasts:

1. "Ear Hustle" - A podcast that shares stories of life inside prison and after, produced by individuals incarcerated at San Quentin State Prison.
2. "The Stoop" - A podcast that explores stories and issues related to the Black experience, with a focus on personal narratives and cultural analysis.
3. "Transformation Talk Radio" - A podcast network featuring shows on personal growth, spirituality, and social change.
4. "Second Chances" - A podcast that shares stories of individuals who have overcome adversity and transformed their lives.
5. "The Reentry Podcast" - A podcast that explores issues related to life after incarceration, with a focus on strategies for successful reentry and advocacy for criminal justice reform.
6. TRIBE BROADCAST MEDIA GROUP Provides movies, podcasts, and music through their website.

These resources are just a starting point, and there are many more books, organizations, and media outlets that can provide valuable information and support. I encourage you to explore, to learn, and to seek out the resources that resonate with your own journey and goals.

Remember, transformation is a lifelong process, and there is always more to discover and grow. By staying open, curious, and engaged, you can continue to build a life of meaning, purpose, and positive impact. And know that you are not alone on this path - there is a whole community of people who are rooting for you and ready to support you along the way.

Acknowledgments

Writing this book has been a profound journey of reflection, healing, and growth, and I could not have done it alone. There are so many people who have supported, inspired, and believed in me along the way, and I want to take a moment to express my deepest gratitude.

First and foremost, I want to thank my family. To my mother and father, who never gave up on me, even in my darkest moments. Your unwavering love, your fierce advocacy, and your unshakable faith in my potential have been the foundation of my transformation. To my siblings, who have been my rocks and my role models. Your resilience, your humor, and your big hearts have carried me through countless challenges and filled my life with joy.

To the mentors and teachers who saw something in me that I couldn't see in myself. To Ms. Johnson, my high school English teacher, who encouraged me to write and believed in my voice. To Dr. Patel, my college advisor, who pushed me to dream big and pursue my passions. To Coach Williams, who taught me the power of discipline and teamwork. Your guidance, your wisdom, and your investment in my growth have been invaluable gifts.

To my colleagues and comrades at the DWU Local 100, who have been my brothers and sisters in struggle and solidarity. Your courage, your commitment, and your tireless fight for justice have inspired me every day. I am so proud to stand alongside you and to be part of a movement that is changing lives and shaping history.

To the young people I have had the privilege to mentor and serve. You have taught me so much about resilience, creativity, and the power of possibility. Your stories, your dreams, and your unbreakable spirits give me hope for the future. Please know that you are not alone, that you are valued, and that you have a community that believes in you and is fighting for you.

To the activists, advocates, and changemakers who are working to build a more just and equitable world. Your vision, your strategy, and your bold leadership are paving the way for transformative change. Thank you for your partnership, your allyship, and your unwavering commitment to the cause.

To the readers who have picked up this book and joined me on this journey. Your willingness to engage, to empathize, and to examine your own lives and communities is a powerful act of transformation in itself. I hope that my story can be a source of inspiration, a call to action, and a reminder of our shared humanity.

And finally, to the ancestors and elders who have paved the way, who have fought and sacrificed and dreamed so that we could have the opportunities we have today. I stand on your shoulders, I carry your legacy, and I pledge to continue the work of building a world where every person can thrive and reach their full potential.

There are so many more people I could name - friends, neighbors, coaches, and countless others who have touched my life in ways big and small. Please know that even if you are not mentioned here by name, your impact and your presence are deeply felt and appreciated.

Writing this book has been a labor of love, a testament to the power of story and the possibility of transformation. I am so grateful to everyone who has been a part of this journey, and I am excited to continue the work of building a beloved community, one relationship, one story, one action at a time.

With deepest gratitude and love,
Stan Scott

About the Man

I am Stan Scott, a longshoreman, labor leader, community advocate, and changemaker. My journey of transformation has inspired countless individuals across the country. Born and raised in Oakland, California, my early life was marked by the challenges and temptations of the streets. As a young man, I struggled with addiction, criminality, and a sense of hopelessness about my future.

But through the power of education, mentorship, and personal determination, I was able to turn my life around. I enrolled in community college, where I discovered a passion for social justice and a talent for leadership. I went on to earn a bachelor's degree in social work and a master's degree in labor studies, becoming the first in my family to graduate from college.

In my work as a longshoreman and a leader in the Dock Workers Union (DWU) Local 100, I have been a tireless advocate for workers' rights, racial justice, and community empowerment. I have served on numerous committees and boards, including the DWU's Coast Safety Committee, the Port of Oakland's Task Force on fatherhood and families , and the Alameda County Juvenile Justice Commission.

But my impact extends far beyond the docks and the union hall. I am also a sought-after speaker, facilitator, and mentor who has shared my story and strategies for change with audiences across the country. I have worked with youth organizations, schools, prisons, and community groups to inspire and empower individuals to transform their lives and their communities.

As a writer, I bring my unique voice and perspective to the page, weaving together personal narrative, social analysis, and practical wisdom. My writing has appeared in publications such as the San Francisco Chronicle, the Oakland Post, and the DWU Dispatcher, and I have been featured in numerous media outlets, including KQED, KPFA, and the East Bay Times.

My commitment to justice and equity has been recognized with numerous awards and honors, including the DWU's Bridges-Robertson-Schmidt Leadership Award, the Oakland City Council's Citizen Humanitarian Award, and the NAACP's Community Service Award. But for me, the true reward is the impact I see every day in the lives of the people I serve and the communities I help to build.

When I'm not working, writing, or organizing, I enjoy spending time with my family, cooking, and exploring the natural beauty of the Bay Area. I am also an avid reader and a lifelong learner who is always seeking new ways to grow and make a difference.

With "From the Corner to the Clock," I hope to share my story and insights with a wider audience, and to inspire readers to embrace the power of transformation in their own lives and communities. I believe that every person has the potential to create positive change, and that by working together, we can build a world where everyone has the opportunity to thrive.

From the Block to the Docks

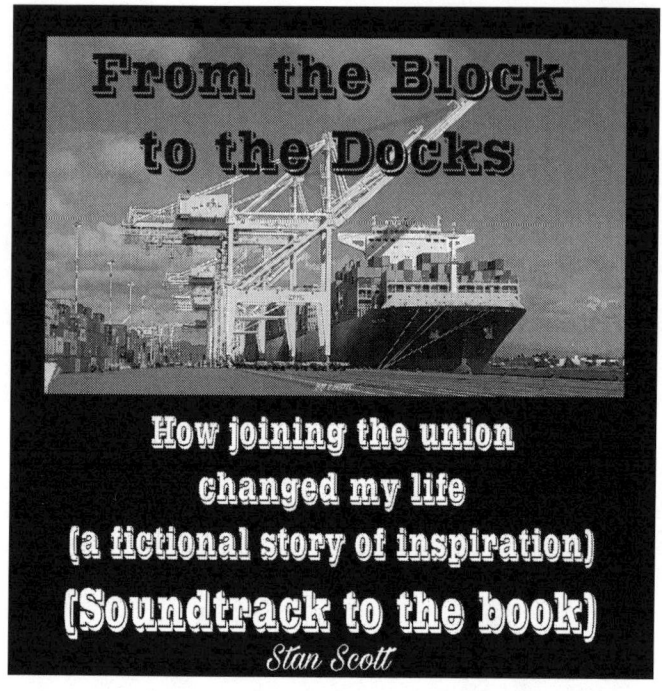

How joining the union changed my life (a fictional story of inspiration) (Soundtrack to the book)

Stan Scott

This is a 5-track Song album that includes the Full Audiobook available on Bandcamp and all streaming platforms
*Available on Amazon Music, YouTube, Spotify, Pandora, Deezer, etc....
*Music available for commercial use at Airbit.com
1. From the Block to the Dockz by S Scott
2. Dockz Elevation By S Scott
3. Blockz 2 Da Dockz By Scott
4. New Dockz Hustle by S Scott

How joining the union changed my life (A fictional story of inspiration)

From the Block to the Docks

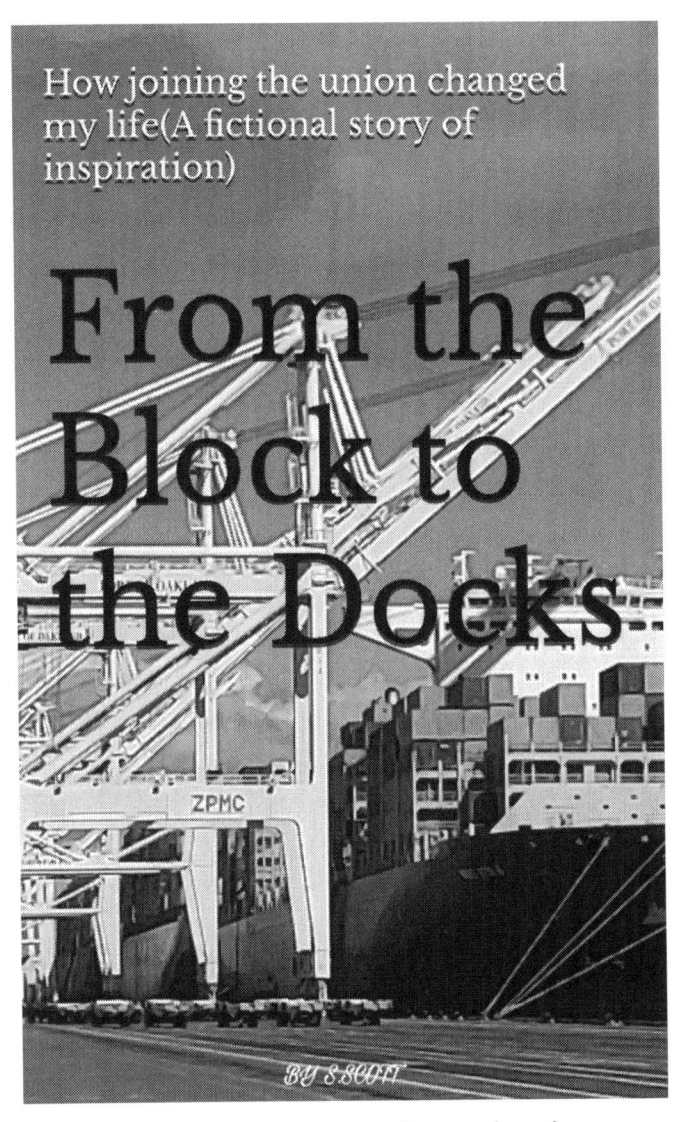

BY S SCOTT

On Kindle and Amazon Paperback
Read aloud version available on GoogleBooks

Available on Google Books, Kindle, and on Amazon Paperback

Mobilizing in OUR OWN NAME

Million Worker March

An Anthology by Clarence Thomas

Cleophas Williams
My Life Story
IN THE INTERNATIONAL LONGSHORE & WAREHOUSE UNION
LOCAL 10

An introduction by
Clarence Thomas

DeClare Publishing

TRIBE BROADCAST MEDIA GROUP

THE FUNK SONATRA PROJECT

A SCI-FI NOVELLA

O.W. SERELLUS

Against All ODDS

Dr. Nichole Pettway Ma, AMFT

A TRIUMPHANT JOURNEY FROM ADDICTION & INCARCERATION

Made in the USA
Columbia, SC
07 July 2024